This book belongs to

_____

© 2006 Big Idea, Inc.

VEGGIETALES®, character names, likenesses, and other indicia
are trademarks of Big Idea, Inc. All rights reserved.

All scripture quotations, unless otherwise indicated, are taken from the
HOLY BIBLE, NEW INTERNATIONAL READER'S VERSION®.
Copyright © 1995, 1996, 1998 by International Bible Society.
All rights reserved.

Published by Scholastic Inc., 90 Old Sherman Turnpike, Danbury, Connecticut 06816.

SCHOLASTIC and associated logos are trademarks and/or
registered trademarks of Scholastic Inc.

This product is available for distribution only through the direct-to-home market.

ISBN: 0-439-87928-0

Printed in the U.S.A.

First Scholastic printing, November 2006

THE Spaghetti WESTERN

A Lesson in
Showing Mercy

by Doug Peterson
Illustrated by Tom Bancroft and Rob Corley
Colored by Jon Conkling

SCHOLASTIC INC.

New York Toronto London Auckland Sydney
Mexico City New Delhi Hong Kong Buenos Aires

"This town ain't big enough for the two of us," Cowboy
Larry snarled at an imaginary villain. Then he reached for his
dodge ball and hurled it right at the wall. But the ball bounced
straight back and knocked Larry flat.

Things like that usually happened whenever Larry practiced
his dodge ball throwing in the sheriff's office.

Bob was getting ready to leave for the Horseshoe Polishing Convention in Buzzard Neck City. While he was gone, Larry would be the sheriff.

"Are you sure you're going to be all right while I'm away?" asked Sheriff Bob.

"Don't worry about me," Larry chirped. "What can **possibly** go wrong?"

Bob stopped to think about all the things that could go wrong with Larry in charge. Fifteen minutes later, Bob dashed out the door. He was late for his stagecoach.

Larry spent the next hour reading Wyatt Slurp comic books. It was a quiet day in Dodge Ball City—until Botch Scallion and the Sunburn Kid stormed into the office.

"Sheriff Larry! Come quickly!" blurted Sunburn.
"There's somebody you have to arrest!"

"Who's the villain?" Larry shouted, leaping from his chair.

"We caught Mayor Nezzer squeezing his toothpaste tube in the middle!" reported Botch Scallion.

Larry looked confused. "Is it against the law to squeeze toothpaste tubes in the middle?" he asked.

"*Of course!*" said Sunburn. "Everyone knows that the tubes are supposed to be squeezed from the end."

"Wyatt Slurp would never let anyone get away with that," added Botch.

"That's true," Larry said. Wyatt Slurp, the most famous sheriff in the West, was always arresting people.

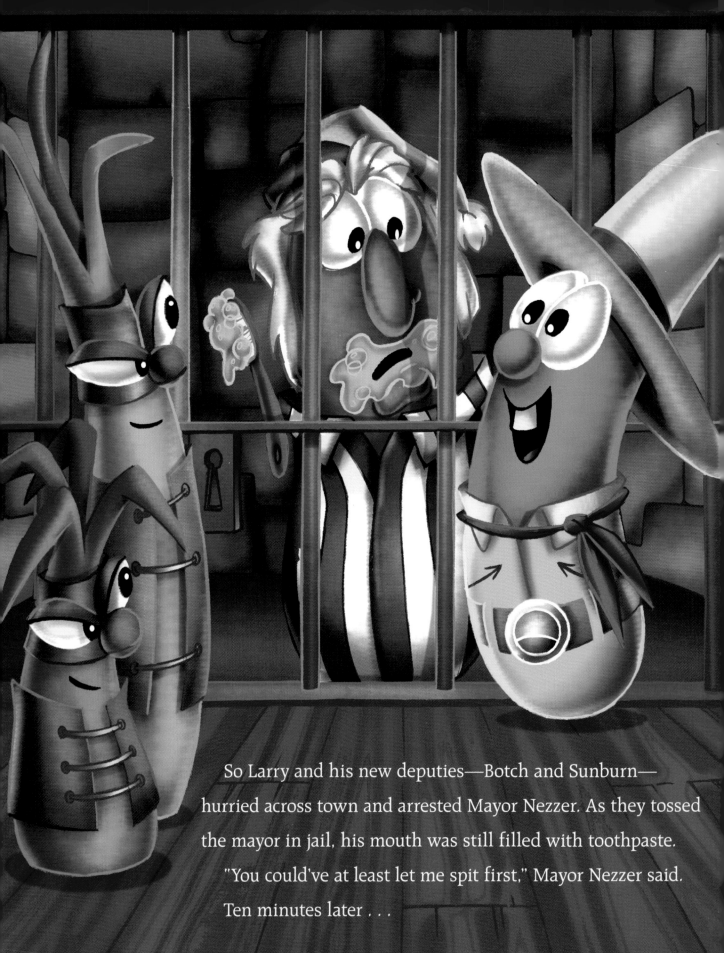

So Larry and his new deputies—Botch and Sunburn—
hurried across town and arrested Mayor Nezzer. As they tossed
the mayor in jail, his mouth was still filled with toothpaste.
"You could've at least let me spit first," Mayor Nezzer said.
Ten minutes later . . .

"**Sheriff Larry!** Come quickly!" It was Botch and Sunburn again. "Archibald Asparagus forgot to return his DVD to the Bronco-Buster video store. Arrest him!"

After the toothpaste crime, Larry thought it was pretty cool throwing people in jail. So he, Botch, and Sunburn arrested Archibald.

But that was only the beginning. They also arrested Madame Blueberry for losing the TV remote.

They nabbed Laura Carrot for letting her cell-phone battery die.

And they tossed two cows in jail for tracking mud on a carpet.

By the next day, the jail cell was bursting at the seams. The sheriff's office wall was covered with Wanted posters. And Botch and Sunburn got a reward for every "criminal" they helped catch.

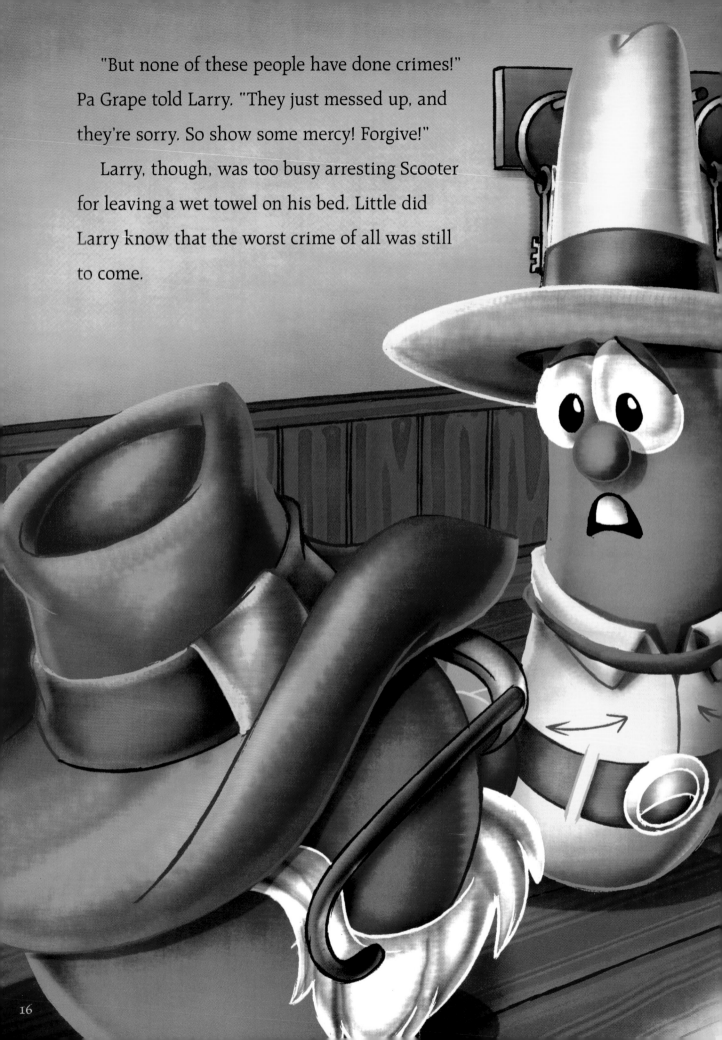

"But none of these people have done crimes!"
Pa Grape told Larry. "They just messed up, and
they're sorry. So show some mercy! Forgive!"

Larry, though, was too busy arresting Scooter
for leaving a wet towel on his bed. Little did
Larry know that the worst crime of all was still
to come.

"**Sheriff Larry! Come quickly!**" shouted Sunburn from the doorway. "Junior Asparagus spilled spaghetti sauce on his vest!"

"How could anyone do something so dastardly?" Larry asked. "Where is he now?"

"Junior and his family slipped out of town!" said Botch. "We have to get a posse together and catch him!"

Ten minutes later, Sheriff Larry
had rounded up three possums.

"Um . . . Sheriff Larry, we said
we needed a *posse*, not possums,"
said Botch. "A posse is a group of
people that tracks down villains."

"Oops," Larry said.

So Larry, Botch, Sunburn, and the three possums saddled up their horses and rode out of town.

The posse finally caught up with the Asparagus family on the Hoppy Trails near Gulp Gulch. The family had stopped for lunch.

"Junior Asparagus, you're under arrest for spilling paghetti sauce," said Larry.

"What are you talking about?" Mr. Asparagus asked. "When Junior spilled the sauce, he told us he was sorry. And we forgave him. That's called showing mercy."

"Wouldn't you want someone to show mercy toward *you* when you mess up?" added Mrs. Asparagus. "Wouldn't you want forgiveness?"

Botch Scallion and the Sunburn Kid looked at each other and laughed. "We don't need mercy," Botch said, "because we *never* mess up."

"Then answer this. If you never mess up, why are you standing in quicksand?" asked Mr. Asparagus.

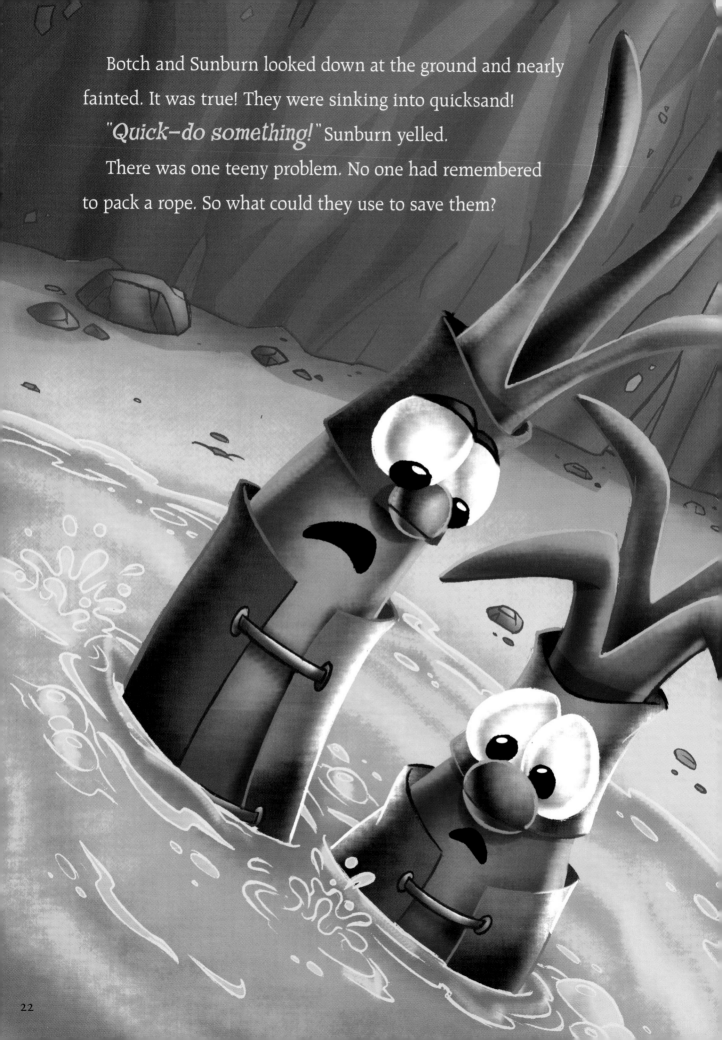

Botch and Sunburn looked down at the ground and nearly fainted. It was true! They were sinking into quicksand!

"*Quick—do something!*" Sunburn yelled.

There was one teeny problem. No one had remembered to pack a rope. So what could they use to save them?

"The spaghetti noodles!" Junior shouted.
"Use spaghetti noodles as rope!"

"Get serious!" said Botch. "How can you use
a spaghetti noodle as a rope?"

"Mr. Lunt, our cook, messed up when he
was making the noodles last night!" said Junior.
"The leftovers are as tough as rope!"

Junior was absolutely right! So Larry tried to tie a long noodle into a lasso—but accidentally tied himself to his horse instead. Then the possums leaped into action. With blazing speed, they made a spaghetti lasso and hurled it to the sinking cowboys.

The possums pulled Botch Scallion and the Sunburn Kid to safety.

From that moment on, Larry realized that *everyone* messes up, including him. But even better, he learned that when people say they're sorry, he should show mercy. After all, God does.

"When we mess up," said Mr. Asparagus, "God reaches out to help us. When we feel like we're sinking, He pulls us back up."

"That's right, God is a rescuer," Mrs. Asparagus added. "He forgives."

Even Botch and Sunburn were beginning to realize that mercy makes sense.

The next day, Sheriff Bob returned to Dodge Ball City. By this time, the jail cell was empty and all the Wanted posters were in the recycling bin.

"Wow!" exclaimed Bob. "I have to hand it to you, Larry. I really didn't think you would make it through these three days without messing up."

"Oh, I messed up some," Larry said, setting aside his comic book. "But the town showed great mercy toward me."

"That's fantastic," said Bob. All in all, he was happy about how things had gone.

In fact, only one thing baffled Bob. Why were three possums in cowboy hats trying to lasso him with spaghetti noodles?

He [God] saved us. It wasn't because of the good
things we had done. It was because of His mercy . . .
Titus 3:5